Also in this series

The Walker Book of Animal Stories
The Walker Book of Funny Stories
The Walker Book of Magical Stories
The Walker Book of Stunning Stories

This collection published 1995 as *A Walker Treasury: Stories for Six-Year-Olds*
and 2000 as *The Walker Book of Stories for 6+ year olds*
by Walker Books Ltd, 87 Vauxhall Walk, London SE11 5HJ

This edition published 2004

2 4 6 8 10 9 7 5 3 1

This book has been typeset in ITC Garamond

Printed and bound in Great Britain
by Creative Print and Design (Wales), Ebbw Vale

British Library Cataloguing in Publication Data:
a catalogue record for this book is
available from the British Library

ISBN 1-84428-463-8

The
Walker Book of

terrific
tales

WALKER BOOKS
AND SUBSIDIARIES
LONDON · BOSTON · SYDNEY · AUCKLAND

CONTENTS

Art, You're Magic!

by SAM McBRATNEY
illustrated by TONY BLUNDELL

Mervyn Magee came to school in a new blue tie.

"I like your tie, Mervyn," everybody said. Even Henrietta Turtle said that she liked Mervyn's tie. Miss Ray, their teacher, said it looked like a lovely big butterfly.

I want a tie like that, thought Art. When Art came home from school he talked to his mother in the kitchen.

"Mummy, will you buy me a butterfly tie for round my neck, please? I want a red one."

At that moment his mother was helping Angela, Art's big sister, to whiten her gym shoes on the tiled floor.

"A butterfly tie?" she said. "What on earth is a butterfly tie?"

"He means a bow tie," said Angela. "He wants to look smart for Henrietta Turtle, don't you, Art?"

Angela knew perfectly well that Art didn't like Henrietta Turtle, but Art decided to ignore her.

"I think people would like me better if I had a butterfly tie," he said.

"My sweet angel," said his mother, "everybody likes you as you are. People would adore you if you ran about in rags."

Angela rolled her eyes. "Lay off, Mum, you'll swell his head."

"Well, it's true. And of course you can have a butterfly tie. *If*," she added, "you promise to keep it good."

Art promised that he would keep it good. And so, when his dad came home that day he found three people waiting for him in the middle of the kitchen – and one of those people was wearing a brand new tie.

"Well, do you notice anything different?" said Mrs Smith.

"By Jove, that's some tie," said Mr Smith.

"Daddy, I picked this tie all by myself. If you want to wear it sometimes, I could lend it to you," shouted Art.

For some reason this made his family laugh.

Art tramped cheerfully up the stairs to look at himself in the mirror again.

Next morning, Art marched into the cloakroom with everybody else in Miss Ray's line. As soon as he took off his coat Henrietta Turtle spotted his new tie.

"Mervyn Magee had one of those ties first," she said, "and you are a copycat, Arthur Smith."

"You shut up," Art said. Henrietta Turtle certainly wasn't one of his friends and she never would be.

"I won't shut up."

"You're not allowed to talk to me."

"I am allowed if it's true. Copycat!"

You are really making me angry, thought Art. He wanted to zap Henrietta Turtle and make her howl, but zapping was not allowed in school, so he said, "Shut up, Big Nose."

"Don't you call me Big Nose!"

Quite a few people had become interested in this battle of words in the cloakroom and Miss Ray was one of them.

"Henrietta Turtle and Arthur Smith, I want to see both of you in your seats right now."

Art went to his seat thinking how Henrietta Turtle should be moved into somebody else's class. She'd nearly got him into Trouble yet again.

After Miss Ray had taken the register, the class practised for their play. Art was a lion in the play.

Although he roared his loudest, Miss Ray did not say what a good lion he was and she did not say how nice his new tie was.

Art was disappointed and blamed Henrietta Turtle for this.

At break, Art's friend Katy asked him if he wanted to eat some of her yogurt.

"I wouldn't give him any yogurt if I was you, Katy," said Henrietta Turtle, "because he's a copycat. Mervyn Magee has a bow tie just like that and he had it first."

Zap, zap! thought Art. Boy, you are really annoying me.

"And another thing," Henrietta Turtle went on, "that tie looks like a big red insect and it's sucking all the blood out of your head."

Art was glad when Henrietta Turtle went away to talk to somebody else.

After break Miss Ray gave her class some number work to do. Everybody had to think hard, especially at Art's table, so there wasn't much noise for a while. Then there was a loud cry.

"Aaaaa! Look what he's done! He's ruined my special giant rubber and it's my only one!"

Three quick-marching strides brought Miss Ray to the table where Art sat with Mervyn Magee, Katy and Henrietta Turtle. She picked up the giant rubber.

"Who wrote BIG NOSE on this rubber?"

Art sucked his top lip and looked down. Mervyn Magee smiled because he loved Trouble, and Katy chewed her pencil anxiously in case the blame should somehow settle on her.

"YOU DID IT, ARTHUR SMITH!" howled Henrietta Turtle.

It was true, he'd done it. Art's head hung low with shame as Miss Ray walked him to the blackboard with these awful words: "Well, I didn't think I had any bad children in my class this year, but I was mistaken, wasn't I? You will stand there for five whole minutes, Arthur Smith, so that everybody can see what happens to people who get up to silly nonsense."

And when they practised their play again, Miss Ray wouldn't let him be a lion. Art was not happy.

When he got home he found his mother having tea with Katy's mum, who lived next door.

"Well, Art," said Katy's mum, "did you dazzle everybody with your new ... what do you call it?"

"Butterfly tie," said Mrs Smith.

"I'm going to zap Henrietta Turtle," he cried, and his eyes were fierce and blue. "I'm going to zap her head off!"

That made the mothers stop smiling. Art didn't care. Up the stairs he went to crawl under the bed and lie there in the peace and quiet with some of his toys.

* * *

All the world seemed far away as Art lay curled up in the half-dark, thinking how this tie, the one round his neck, was a stupid tie. I don't want it any more, he decided.

A familiar sound reached his ears. In the garden next door, Katy's yappy dog was barking. Art began to bark too, as if he understood dog-talk.

And then a wonderful idea came into his head and all of a sudden he knew what to do with his tie – the very thing! As fast as he could go, Art raced down the stairs and out into the garden to where the fence was lowest. Peanuts looked up at him, wagging his tail.

"Yappy dog," Art called quietly.

"Rrrrrrruf!"

"I've got something for you here," said Art, climbing over the fence into Katy's garden.

Yappy dog Peanuts had never seen a butterfly tie before and he didn't seem to want one – Art had some trouble fitting it round his neck. At last the job was done, and what a difference that tie made to tatty old Peanuts! Below the straggly whiskers that poked about in the dirt all day could now be seen a splendid dash of butterfly-shaped colour. Peanuts, though, had grown tired of this nonsense, and took off like a hare round the corner of Katy's house.

And the butterfly tie went with him!

Ding-dong! ding-dong!

Art heard the doorbell plainly from upstairs, where he sat in bed talking to some furry animals.

"Art. Arthur Smith! Come down those stairs at once."

Dad's voice! Was this Trouble? When Art went into the living-room he saw the red tie dangling from his dad's hand. It was dirty; it hung in tatters; it was all chewed up.

"Jeepers, Dad!" said Angela. "Is that the new tie?"

"It *was*," said Mr Smith.

"The twit must have been wearing it round his welly boot," cried Angela.

Don't you dare call me a twit, thought Art. But he could see that this was Trouble, all right.

"A little while ago," said Mr Smith, "Katy's mum saw Peanuts the dog down at the shops with something round his neck that looked like a tie. That

can't be *Art's* tie, she said to herself, Art is wearing his new tie. But it *was* his tie. She found it later on the back step. And here it is!"

"You stuck your new tie on that scruffy beast?" cried Angela.

"I thought it was his birthday," Art mumbled.

"Nuts!" cried Angela. "Dogs do not have birthdays. One dog's day is like any other, and they can't count. There's something wrong with your brain, Arthur Smith."

"You stop talking to me," said Art.

But there was plenty of talking to be done and Mr Smith did most of it as he trailed Art back to bed. He was still talking about the price of clothes, and about the boys and girls in the world who couldn't afford to buy food never mind new ties, as he tucked Art in for the night.

Mum came in to say night-night, and held up the lion's tail she'd made for him. "You'd better not forget this in the morning," she said, and put out the light.

I don't want to go to school and I don't want to be a lion and everybody's cross with me, thought Art. People blame me for everything. How many times had Miss Ray smiled at him all day? Not once. Art reached out an arm and dragged Big Bendy into bed with him, his true friend, and lay down to sleep. Was it true, he wondered, that dogs didn't have birthdays?

*　　*　　*

Next morning Art went off to school with his lion's tail carefully folded up in his school bag.

This was an important Friday morning because Miss Ray's class was putting on a play for the other infant classes. Quite a few mothers were coming to watch it too, including Art's.

The play was a very good story – Art was sure that people would enjoy it. Once there was a bad king and this bad king put Daniel into the cave with lions. He thought the lions would eat Daniel, but they didn't. God sent an angel – Katy – and the angel made the lions close their mouths. They couldn't hurt Daniel, and he was safe.

So, at ten past nine, the children from the other classes came out of their rooms and walked down to the Hall. Here they sat in rows and waited for Miss Ray's class to come in and do their play.

The people in the Hall didn't know that there was a problem. Ernie wasn't here. He was at home in bed. Miss Ray had no Daniel!

"What am I going to *do*?" she said to Katy's mum, who was there to pin on Katy's angel wings. "How can I have a play about Daniel without a *Daniel*; why did he pick *this* Friday to get the chicken-pox?"

"Maybe you could do the play next week," said Katy's mum.

All the children began to groan.

Then Miss Ray felt someone prodding her with a lion's mask.

"I can be Daniel," said a voice – she looked down, and there was Art.

"Can you? Can you really? Do you know the words?"

"I know everybody's words," said Art.

"He does, Miss Ray," said Katy, "he knows everybody's words. He said them all to me when we were going home from school."

"Then we'll try it!" cried Miss Ray. "Quick, get him dressed."

There wasn't a moment to lose because everybody in the Hall was waiting. Katy's mum took off Art's tail and dressed him up in Daniel's clothes – a towel for his head and a stripy pyjama top.

Then all the lions and the bad king and Daniel and the angel hurried up the corridor as fast as they could go.

When Art got up on the stage in front of everybody that Friday morning he waved to his mum to make sure she knew he wasn't a lion any more. And then the play began.

The best moment came when the bad king pushed Daniel among the lions, who walked round in a circle and began to roar. Art looked down at all the children who were watching, and he knew what they were thinking – they were thinking that he would soon be eaten.

Now it was time for Katy to say her words. She had to tell the lions to close their mouths and leave Daniel alone.

But she didn't. Katy couldn't. She was afraid to speak in front of all those people.

The lions were going wild! Henrietta Turtle, who was definitely the best lion, was roaring her head off and waving her mask about. The play was going to be ruined if Katy didn't speak!

Art walked across the stage and put an arm round her shoulder. "You'd better shut them up or Henrietta Turtle is going to eat me," he said.

Katy looked at Henrietta and saw that this was true. She waved an arm in the air – a very angry angel.

"Shut your mouth, Henrietta Turtle!" she called out.

Her words worked like magic.

Henrietta Turtle closed her lips and sucked them into her mouth, as if she had no teeth. Then she stuck her hands under her armpits to show that her fierce paws didn't work, either. All the lions did the same and they looked like pet mice. Daniel was saved and the play was over.

Everybody clapped and clapped. Art's mum was one of those who clapped the longest and he could see that she'd forgotten all the Trouble caused by that stupid tie.

In the corridor Miss Ray swept Art off his feet and gave him quite a strong cuddle.

"Arthur Smith, you are magic," she said. "I have never seen a more wonderful Daniel and I think you're just great."

Art hoped that Henrietta Turtle was listening.

Vicky Fox

by BERLIE DOHERTY
illustrated by KIM LEWIS

Deep in the earth it was brown and cool, and it smelled of mushrooms and leaves. In the spinney woods a fox watched for the moonlight and streaked out from his lair. He put his snout to the ground to sniff out the trails he had made his own. He crossed the scents of rabbits and badgers and all the other creatures of the night. He smelled cats and dogs and human beings. He smelled the egg-man's hens in the field at the edge of town.

In his lair his vixen lay with her brush-tail tucked under her chin. She watched for the fox to bring her food. Her brown cubs nuzzled each other, snug at her side and warm with her milk.

In the houses children were sleeping. In the house in the field at the edge of town a little girl called Ruth opened her eyes and listened. She could hear the hens screeching in the yard. She heard her father, the egg-man, getting out of his bed, and she heard the stairs creaking. "I'll get that fox!" she heard him say. "This time I'll get him, good and proper."

Ruth heard him going out to the yard. She could hear him untying the dogs.

"You shouldn't, you shouldn't," the little girl cried. "Killing the lovely foxes is cruel."

And that was the night that the fox died. The dogs ran out to meet him, and he never went home again. The dogs ran on to the vixen's lair and found the vixen with her brush tucked under her chin. They found the nuzzling cubs that were warm with her milk by her side. And when the egg-man whistled them home they left them all for dead.

But one of the cubs was still alive. She whimpered for her mother to give her milk. She whimpered for her brothers and sisters to nuzzle her. She whimpered for her father to come home. But nobody answered her.

The moon went dark, and all night long it rained. The rain hissed like long snakes, and all the leaves pattered and gleamed.

The fox cub curled up with the brush tucked under her chin and waited for food.

Fox in a box

Next morning the egg-man went across the field to see what his dogs had done.

Well, he thought, these foxes won't be after my hens again, that's for sure. He was just about to go when one of the fox cubs opened her eyes, and the egg-man saw that she was still alive. She was no bigger than a kitten, and she was as brown as a nut. She panted up at him with fright. He remembered what his daughter Ruth had said in the night. "You shouldn't, you shouldn't," she had cried. "Killing the lovely foxes is cruel."

The egg-man picked up the fox cub by the scruff of her neck and tucked her under his arm so she wouldn't bite him. He took her into the house and put her down on the table.

31

"If you think killing foxes is wrong," he said to Ruth, "then make this one live."

Ruth had no idea what to do with a fox. She put her in a box and fed her on milk and food scraps. She called her Vicky Fox. She daren't touch her, because her mouth was always open and her little rows of teeth were sharp and fine. She daren't stroke her or pick her up. But she thought the fox cub was so beautiful that she couldn't take her eyes off her. She just couldn't stop looking at her. She watched her for hours, and Vicky Fox curled up in her box and never took her eyes off Ruth.

Sometimes, when Ruth went out of the room, the cub would sneak out of the box and run across the carpet, run up and down the furniture, run under the table. But as soon as the door opened she would sneak back into her box and lie there, panting with fear, waiting for food, and watching.

She grew bigger and stronger, and her coat that was as brown as a nut turned a deep and rusty red, like oak leaves in autumn. Her eyes were like amber beads. She was beautiful. But Ruth daren't touch Vicky Fox in case she snapped her hand off, and she hated her smell.

"Put her out," the egg-man said. "The dogs won't get her now. They're too used to her. And she won't get the hens. She doesn't know how to hunt. Let her go."

"But I like having a fox for a pet," said Ruth.

Vicky Fox curled up and watched her, panting with fear.

"What good is a pet that you're scared of, and that makes the house smell like a farmyard?" the egg-man said. "Wild things don't make pets. Let her go."

"Will she die, if I let her go?" Ruth asked, and her father laughed.

"Of course she will," he said.

Wily Ruth

But Ruth was wily. She put Vicky Fox out, but she didn't let her go. She put her box in a shed that her father never used. Cobwebs hung from the beams like old men's beards. Vicky Fox crawled under a wheelbarrow and peered out at Ruth. Her eyes were as bright as yellow lamps. Her tiny teeth gleamed. She panted with fright. Ruth closed the bottom door of the shed and watched her. She threw in some chicken scraps and Vicky Fox

pushed them with her snout till they were hidden under a pile of straw.

"You're no good for a pet, you aren't," Ruth told her through the top door of the shed. "But remember who your friend is, Vicky Fox. You'd have died if I hadn't fed you and given you a home."

Vicky Fox slunk into the shadows under the old wheelbarrow. She lay there, panting.

"Nobody else loves you, Vicky Fox, remember that," Ruth said. She ran back through the yard, where the brown and red hens clucked round her feet and bobbed about for grain.

When the yard was quiet, Vicky Fox crept from her box. She lay still. It grew dark outside. Rain came down, and she could hear it, hissing like snakes. She listened for her mother to give her milk, and for her brothers and sisters to nuzzle her, and for her father to come loping home, but nobody came.

The visitors

Then one day somebody tried to help Vicky Fox, but she did it all wrong. This is what happened.

It was a day that was full of the end of summer.

You know what it's like, when the sky is blue but there's mist in the air. When the leaves are turning to gold on the trees. When the cobwebs are hanging with dew all day. That was the day the visitors came and one of them tried to help Vicky Fox, and she got it all wrong.

Ruth was sitting in her yard with the hens. She heard voices out in the lane, and she went to the gate to see who it was. She could see an old lady with hair like wool holding a little girl by the hand. The old lady had a stick, and the girl had a box. They were picking blackberries from the hedge.

The old lady saw Ruth watching them from the gate and she called out to her. "Do you want to pick blackberries with us?"

Ruth ducked down to the hens so she couldn't be seen. She was a little bit scared of Old Miss Annie because she'd noticed how twiggy and twisted her hands were. But she liked her whispery voice. It made her think of morning mist on her field.

She didn't like Willa because she held Old Miss Annie's hand as if she just didn't care how twisted it was.

Ruth said in a voice like a hen's, all clucky and high, "There's plenty more blackberries in the field, you know," and she ran and hid behind Vicky Fox's shed.

Old Miss Annie stopped by the gate. "So there are," she said. "Beautiful blackberries, big and fat and bursting with juice, Willa." Then she said in a voice loud enough for Ruth to hear, "Doesn't the egg-girl's mother want them for jam?"

"She hasn't got a mother," Ruth said in a voice like a hen. She liked the way Old Miss Annie said "jam", making the word sound runny and sticky and sweet.

"Well, I'll make some for her and her father if she'll help me pick blackberries from her field," Old Miss Annie said, and Ruth came out from behind the shed, a little bit shy, and opened the gate for them.

As they came into the field Old Miss Annie stopped and sniffed.

"Fox!" she said. "I can smell fox around here."

"She's my pet," Ruth said. "Vicky Fox."

"Where is she then?" asked Willa, who didn't believe for a minute that Ruth could have a fox, even if she was the egg-man's daughter and lived in a house in a field.

Ruth opened the top door of the shed and Willa

stood on her tiptoes and they all peered into its darkness.

Run, Vicky Fox!

As soon as Vicky Fox heard the voices of strangers she jumped up on the beam of her shed. She ran backwards and forwards along it, backwards and forwards in the shadows among the cobwebs that hung like old men's beards. Her snout was down and sniffing her tracks. Her amber eyes gleamed as she watched Willa and Old Miss Annie and Ruth. Her mouth was wide open and ready to snap. She was panting with fear.

"She's beautiful," Old Miss Annie said. Ruth nudged closer to her, and Willa had to move sideways. She didn't like Ruth one bit.

"And does Vicky Fox live here all the time?" Old Miss Annie asked.

"Yes," said Ruth. "She's my pet."

"Oh, dear," said Old Miss Annie.

"Can I stroke her?" asked Willa.

"You'd better not try," said Ruth. "Or she'll have you for her tea."

Miss Annie sighed. "I wish Vicky Fox could have a run," she said in a tiny faraway voice that seemed to be thinking of woodlands.

And that was when Willa decided to help Vicky Fox, but she got it all wrong.

Old Miss Annie and Ruth started to pick the blackberries on the hedges. Willa trailed behind. She didn't like Ruth because Miss Annie had given her the blackberry box to hold, and that was Willa's job. But Miss Annie's heart wasn't in blackberry picking.

"Look at the tracks in the grass that the animals have made," she said. "Badgers and rabbits and probably foxes, too. Poor Vicky Fox, stuck in a shed when there's all this grass and fox-scent in the air! What a shame!"

"She'd have died if I hadn't fed her!" said Ruth, and when Miss Annie looked down and saw Ruth getting ready to cry she held out her hand. Even though it was twisted and knobbled like sticks, Ruth held it and found how soft and warm it was.

Willa snatched up the box and ran to the other side of the field and stuffed it with blackberries till it was ready to spill.

Before they left the field Old Miss Annie went to Ruth's house. She wanted to thank the egg-man for letting her come into the field, though he was busy counting his money in the kitchen and didn't even know she had been.

"I'll make you some jam!" Old Miss Annie called through the door. "And you and Ruth can have it for your tea."

And it was while Miss Annie was talking at the door that Willa did what she did. She thought she was helping Vicky Fox, but she got it all wrong. She did it to please Old Miss Annie. And she did it because she didn't like Ruth, who was holding Miss Annie's hand.

It didn't take long to do. She opened the bottom door of the shed. And she said, "Run, Vicky Fox. Run!"

Back to the spinney wood

At first nothing happened. The egg-man was going to town and he gave them a lift to their road in his van, and on the way Old Miss Annie fell asleep, so Willa couldn't tell her then. When they arrived Miss Annie went straight to her house to make the jam and Willa had to go home for a bath, so she couldn't tell her then. She didn't tell anyone because she wanted Miss Annie to be the first in the world to know that she had given Vicky Fox a run. When she went to bed she dreamt of her streaking like wildfire through the dark woods, running with the other foxes through the night.

But it didn't happen like that. Long after Willa had gone, Vicky Fox stepped out of her shed. She took her time. She sniffed every bin in the yard. She sniffed at the cat, who just rolled away from her and wasn't afraid. She sniffed at the hens, who pecked and bobbed around her paws for grain. Then, sniffing every blade of grass, she started to cross the field. She crouched so low you would think she was melting into the earth. And through the bushes she went, through the blackberry brambles, and into the spinney woods.

During the night it rained. It hissed down like snakes, and the grass gleamed with it. Vicky Fox crouched down into the roots of trees, afraid. She remembered her mother's milk, and whimpered for it. She whimpered for her brothers and sisters to nuzzle her. She whimpered for her father to come home. She remembered the barking and snarling dogs and she panted with fear. The night moved with fear. Mice scampered across the grass. Rabbits thudded into their burrows. Vicky Fox watched and listened and smelled the animal air. She waited for someone to come and bring her food, but nobody came.

And in her room in the house in the field Ruth lay awake and cried. Her fox had gone.

Willa tells Old Miss Annie

Willa had to go to school next day. At tea-time Old Miss Annie came round with a jar of blackberry jam for her.

"This is the best jam I've ever made!" she said. "And every time I eat it, I'm going to think of Ruth the egg-girl and Vicky Fox."

That was when Willa remembered what she had done. "Miss Annie!" she said, her voice sticky with bread and jam. "Guess what I did!"

She knew how pleased Miss Annie would be.

She licked all her fingers one by one. And then, because Old Miss Annie still hadn't guessed, she said, "I gave Vicky Fox a run!"

She waited for Old Miss Annie to say how pleased she was.

But she didn't. She went quiet and sad.

"Aren't you pleased, Miss Annie?"

"No, Willa, I'm not."

Old Miss Annie held Willa's hands and told her that Vicky Fox might die. "She can't hunt for food. She's never been taught. She's a house fox, Willa. She'll never be able to live in the wild."

"But you said... Oh, Miss Annie, you said that you wished Vicky Fox could have a run!" Willa could hardly speak, she was so afraid for Vicky Fox.

Come home, Vicky Fox

Old Miss Annie shook her head. "Not that sort of run, Willa. Not a running-free run. I meant the sort of run that pet rabbits have. She'd have to have fences six feet high so she couldn't jump over them. And six feet deep so she couldn't dig under them. That's the sort of run that I meant, Willa."

Willa closed her eyes and cried.

Old Miss Annie and Willa hurried down to the

egg-man's house. It was quite a long way, but they both ran for part of it. By the time they arrived they were puffing and out of breath. There was the house in the field, and there was the shed with the bottom door open, and there was Ruth, sitting outside it, waiting for Vicky Fox to come home.

They all went round and round the field calling out Vicky Fox's name. They looked under all the bushes and in all the caves the tree roots made and wherever the grass was high enough to hide a fox.

Then Willa crawled under a bramble bush and into the spinney woods and there she found her.

The fox was curled right round with her brush tucked under her chin. Her mouth was open wide and her little sharp teeth were gleaming white. Her eyes were like amber. She was panting with fright.

"I've found her! I've found her!" Willa shouted. "I've found Vicky Fox!"

Old Miss Annie and Ruth crawled after her. Vicky Fox shrank back into the dark roots.

"She's frightened," said Old Miss Annie. "She's hungry and frightened, and she might bite. But leave her to me, Ruth, and I'll get her home safe."

Ruth and Willa crawled back out of the brambles and sat looking at the see-through moon that was coming into the sky even though the sun was still shining.

"You go to my school," said Ruth.

"Do I?" said Willa.

"I saw you this morning," said Ruth. "But I didn't play with you because I've been crying all night."

"I don't play with anyone," said Willa.

"Neither do I," said Ruth. "Nobody plays with me because I'm an egg-girl. They say I smell of hens."

"You do a bit," agreed Willa. "Nobody plays with me because I talk funny."

"You do a bit," agreed Ruth.

They both stared ahead. The moon was bigger now. Nearly white.

"Anyway," said Willa. "Miss Annie's my friend."

"Vicky Fox is mine," said Ruth.

They could hear Old Miss Annie talking to Vicky Fox as if she were a baby, soft and quiet in her tiny, whispery voice. After a long time of just sitting quietly she knelt forward and reached out her hand to Vicky Fox. She picked her up by the scruff of her neck. She tucked her into her arms and held her jaw so she wouldn't bite. And she carried her over the field to her box in the shed.

*   *   *

Happy ending

You might think *that* is the end of the story, but it isn't quite. Next day Willa and Old Miss Annie went to the house in the field again. They had a jar of blackberry jam for the egg-man, and he was so pleased that he gave them a box of eggs. Miss Annie had something else in her bag. It was a dog collar and a very long clothes-line.

"What are you going to do with that?" Ruth asked her.

"I'm going to give Vicky Fox a run," said Miss Annie.

It took her a long time to fasten the collar round Vicky Fox's neck, a lot of whisperings and shushings in her tiny voice. Then she fastened the clothes-line to the collar and told Willa to open the bottom door of the shed.

And out into the field they went. Vicky Fox darted from scent to scent. She could smell mice and badgers and rabbits. She could smell her own tracks. She crouched into the long grasses, and into the caves that the tree roots made, and under the brambly bushes. She rolled and ran, and always she kept her eyes on Miss Annie. Willa and Ruth had a go, tying the rope to their wrist, and they shrieked

with laughter as Vicky Fox pulled them from one
side of the field to the other.

At last, when they'd all had enough, they led

Vicky Fox back to the shed and untied her rope. She dived into the straw in her box, safe and warm. And almost at once she fell asleep, snoring.

Now every day Old Miss Annie comes to the field. She takes Vicky Fox for a run. It looks more as if Vicky Fox is taking Old Miss Annie for a run, the way she pulls her from one side of the field to the other, to the long grass and the roots of the trees and the brambly bushes where all the smells are rich.

Sometimes Willa comes with her. And when she does she runs in the field behind Old Miss Annie and Vicky Fox – playing with Ruth, her best friend.

Shaleen Goes Swimming

by NADYA SMITH
illustrated by ROBERTA MANSELL

It was the start of the new school year, and the children in Shaleen's class were now Top Infants.

The Top Infants had desks with lids that could open and close, not just a table to sit at. They borrowed books from the library van which came on Tuesdays, but best of all, they went swimming.

Every week, a bus would come at half past nine and take the Top Infants and some junior children to the local swimming baths. There was a big pool for the swimmers, and a smaller, shallow pool for the beginners. All the beginners had blow-up armbands and a float, so that nobody had to worry about sinking.

"You must bring a carrier bag with a swimming costume and a cap and a towel," Miss Harris, their new teacher told them. "If you don't bring them, you might not be able to go, so don't forget."

At dinner-time, Shaleen ran all the way home to tell her mother and father, but when her father heard about it he said, "I'm sorry Shaleen, but you can't go swimming."

"Why not?" asked Shaleen. She felt like bursting into tears. "Everybody can go – Miss Harris said so. And you don't have to pay."

"It's not right for a Muslim girl to take her clothes off in a public place – you know that, Shaleen."

Shaleen looked at her mother, but her mother just said, "You must do what your father says, Shaleen. He knows what is best for you."

*   *   *

When Shaleen got to school the next day, she told Miss Harris, who was very sorry. "Ask your father to come and see me," she said. "Perhaps I could make him change his mind."

Shaleen's father came to the school at half past three. "You must understand," he told Miss Harris, "it is against our religion for girls to take their clothes off in a public place. I don't wish my daughter to do that."

"But there are only schoolchildren at the baths when we go," said Miss Harris. "No one else can come in when we're there. And we asked the people at the Mosque; they said it was all right for small girls to go swimming. Even the Imam's daughter goes, and she's nearly ten."

"People must do what they think is right," said Shaleen's father. "As for me, I do not wish Shaleen to go."

Miss Harris said, "Well, of course, if that is what you want, then she won't go swimming. But may she go with the rest of the class and watch? There will be no one to look after her at school."

"Yes, she may go and watch," said Shaleen's father. "But she must not take her clothes off."

*　　*　　*

The next Wednesday, the bus came and took everyone with their carrier bags to the baths. They went into the changing rooms and put on their costumes, then they all had a hot shower and made sure that their feet were clean. All the beginners lined up at the edge of the pool, and Mrs Reeves, who looked after the children when they were sick or unhappy and who knew all about First Aid, put on their arm bands and blew them up and gave each one a float.

Miss Harris said, "All right – you can go in now!"

A few of the children, who had been to the baths before with older brothers or sisters, jumped in straight away; but most of them had never even seen a pool before, and they went down the steps very slowly and carefully, holding on to the bar at the side. But everybody liked it in the water, and soon they were shouting and jumping about and splashing each other.

Shaleen sat on a wooden bench at the side of the pool; she felt very sad and left out. She felt very hot, too, in her thick coat, but she didn't take it off, remembering what her father had said. Children called to her from the pool, "It's lovely, Shaleen! I wish you could come in, too!"

"Look, I can float!"

"It's really warm!"

After a while, Miss Harris went to talk to the teacher who was looking after the juniors in the big pool, and Mrs Reeves went to the deep end of the little pool, to help some children who were trying to swim. At the other end of the pool, where Shaleen was sitting, there were some wide steps leading down into the water. Some of the children were sitting on the top step, paddling their feet and just playing and talking.

"Poor Shaleen! I wish you could come in," called her friend Sarah.

Shaleen said nothing, but after a few moments she got up and went to the steps and sat on the top step with her feet in the water.

"Shaleen!" cried Sarah. "Look at your shoes and socks – they're soaking! What will Miss Harris say?"

Shaleen didn't answer. She paddled her feet and watched the water pouring out of her shoes when she lifted them up. Then she moved down to the second step. She was sitting in water now, and her wet silk trousers stuck tightly to her legs. The other children crowded round.

"Ooh, Shaleen – you're going to get into trouble, look at your coat!"

Still, Shaleen didn't say a word, but slowly moved down to the next step. The water came up to her waist now. It filled her coat pockets and made her dress feel all tight and clingy. She moved her hands about gently, making patterns in the blue water. The other children moved away – they wanted to go and play where the water was deeper.

Shaleen was left alone. With a little smile, she moved down to the fourth and bottom step, and put her head back so that her long black hair floated on the water like seaweed. She kicked her legs up and splashed. She was soaking wet from the top of her head to her toes.

While Shaleen lay there in the water, Miss Harris returned. She came running along the side of the pool shouting, "Shaleen! Shaleen! What are you doing? You naughty girl – get out at once! You know your father said you were not to go swimming!"

Slowly, Shaleen stood up. She tipped the water out of her pockets, and looked at Miss Harris. "But I didn't take my clothes off," she said.

"Oh, my goodness!" said Miss Harris. "Whatever next!" She had to go and fetch a big towel and wrap Shaleen in it. Then everybody else got out of the

pool and changed into their clothes, and they all went back to school in the bus.

When they got back, Mrs Reeves took Shaleen to find her some dry clothes. She had to find her a vest and knickers and socks and trousers, and a dress and a cardigan, and even a coat and shoes. She wrung the water out of Shaleen's own clothes and put them to dry on the radiators.

As soon as Shaleen's mother came through the gate at half past three, pushing Shaleen's baby sister in the push chair, she said, "Those aren't your clothes, Shaleen! Where are the clothes you had on this morning?"

Mrs Reeves had put all the wet clothes in a carrier bag. Shaleen handed it to her mother without a word. Miss Harris said, "I'm very very sorry. I'm afraid Shaleen went in the water."

"But I didn't take my clothes off," said Shaleen.

"No – she didn't take her clothes off," said Miss Harris. "And that's why they're all in the carrier bag."

They all looked at Shaleen's mother, to see if she was going to be very cross, but she just smiled and said, "Do you really want to go swimming so much, Shaleen?"

Shaleen said, "Yes – yes I do!"

"Well, I'll speak to your father tonight," said her mother, "and then we'll see."

Shaleen's father brought her to school the next day. Her mother had washed and ironed the clothes that she had borrowed, and put them neatly in the carrier bag.

"Thank you very much," Miss Harris said, taking it from him, "I'm sorry about what happened. I should have watched her more carefully."

"That's all right," said Shaleen's father. "There's no harm done. She's a good girl. I told her she must keep her clothes on, and so she did. I just didn't think – " he began to laugh – "I didn't think she would go swimming in her coat and shoes!"

Miss Harris laughed too. "I'm so glad you're not angry with her. She's always very good at school."

Shaleen's father said, "Tell me, is it true that Shaleen is the only girl in the class who is not allowed to go swimming?"

"Yes," Miss Harris said.

"And is it true that when you are at the baths, there are only children there?"

"Indeed it is. And only children from our own school."

"Hmm!" Shaleen's father stroked his beard. "And who looks after them?"

"Myself – Mrs Reeves – Mrs Grant."

"I see." He smiled, and turned to go. "I shall think about it, and let you know."

Nobody spoke about swimming for the rest of the week, although everyone wanted to know what Shaleen's father would decide. Miss Harris didn't want to ask Shaleen, in case the answer was no. But the next Wednesday, when all the children came in with their carrier bags, Shaleen had a carrier bag too. Inside was a black swimming costume, and a towel, and a yellow cap.

Miss Harris said, "Oh, I *am* glad, Shaleen!" and everyone shouted, "Hurrah! Shaleen's going swimming!"

The Finger-eater

by DICK KING-SMITH
illustrated by ARTHUR ROBINS

Long long ago, in the cold lands of the North, there lived a most unusual troll.

Like all the hill-folk (so called because they usually made their homes in holes in the hills) he was hump-backed and bow-legged, with a frog-face and bat-ears and razor-sharp teeth.

But he grew up (though, like all other trolls, not
very tall) with an extremely bad habit – he liked to
eat fingers!

Ulf (for that was his name) always went about
this in the same way. Whenever he spied someone
walking alone on the hills, he would come up,

smiling broadly and hold out a hand, and say politely, "How do you do?"

Now trolls are usually rude and extremely grumpy and don't care how anyone does, so the person would be pleasantly surprised at meeting such a jolly troll, and would hold out his or her hand to shake Ulf's.

Then Ulf would take it and, quick as a flash, bite off a finger with his razor-sharp teeth and run away as fast as his bow-legs would carry him, chewing like mad and grinning all over his frog-face.

Strangers visiting those parts were amazed to see how many men, women and children were lacking a finger on their right hand, especially children, because their fingers were tenderer and much sought after by Ulf.

Nobody lacked more than one finger, because even small children weren't foolish enough to shake hands if they met Ulf a second time, but ran away with them deep in their pockets.

It was usually the index finger that Ulf nipped off because it was the easiest to get at, so that many children grew up pointing with a middle finger …

and holding a pencil between middle and third …

but sometimes Ulf went for the little one: thumbs, for some reason, he did not seem to fancy.

Strangely, the people of those lands were tolerant and long-suffering and seemed to put up with Ulf's bad habit.

"What can't be cured must be endured," they would say, and since they considered it was no use crying over spilt milk, they wasted no tears over lost fingers but got on with their lives with only seven.

* * *

Who knows how long Ulf the troll might have continued in his wicked ways if it had not been for a little girl named Gudrun.

Gudrun was the only child of a reindeer farmer. She had golden hair which she wore in a long plait, and eyes the colour of cornflowers.

Indeed she was as pretty as a picture, looking as though reindeer butter wouldn't melt in her mouth.

She was also a sensible child, who paid attention to what her parents told her.

One evening, as they all sat round the fire outside

their tent, Gudrun's mother said to her, "Remember, you must never shake hands with a troll."

She stirred the cooking-pot that was suspended above the flames. The hand that held the ladle had no little finger.

With his right hand, whose index finger was missing, Gudrun's father picked up a stick to put on the fire.

"What should I do, then?" said Gudrun.

"Put your hands in your pockets and run," he said.

"But why," said Gudrun, "didn't either of you do that?"

"When we were both children," said her mother, "we didn't know about the Finger-eater."

"We were among the first in this district," said her father, "to lose a finger. But now everybody knows."

"Why don't all the mothers and fathers warn their children then?" said Gudrun.

"They do," said her mother, "but sometimes the children don't listen, or they just forget. Mind you remember."

Gudrun thought deeply about this while she was

out on the hills, helping her father herd his reindeer as they grazed their way across the slopes.

It's all very well, she thought, to tell children not to get their fingers eaten, but someone ought to tell that troll not to eat them. Eating people's fingers is wrong.

And being not only a very pretty but also a very resolute child, she resolved that she would stop the Finger-eater. But how?

"Father," she said as she sat milking one of the reindeer, "how big is a troll?"

"No taller than you, Gudrun," her father said, "but much, much stronger."

"Have you ever met one?"

For answer her father held up his right hand.

"Oh, yes," said Gudrun. "But since then, I mean?"

"No," said her father, "but I have quite often seen the hill-folk, just for a moment. Then they scuttle down their holes, for they are all shy of people. Except Ulf the Finger-eater."

"You have never seen him again?"
"No, and nor will you, I hope."
But not long after, Gudrun did.

*   *   *

Even in those bleak Northern lands there are days in the short summer which are bright and warm and flower-filled, and on such a morning Gudrun's father handed her a flask. It was made of reindeer skin, was this flask, and it was stopped with a cork made out of reindeer horn, and it was filled with fresh, rich reindeer milk.

"Be a good girl and take this to your mother," her father said, for the herd's grazing grounds were not far from the family tent, and it did not occur to him that she might come to any harm.

Gudrun set off across the hill, carrying the flask in her right hand. Before she had gone far she saw, in a steep bank, a large hole.

Could that be the home of one of the hill-folk? she thought, and no sooner had she thought it than out of the hole came a hump-backed, bow-legged figure with a frog-face and bat-ears.

Straight towards her he came, his mouth agape in a friendly smile, his hand outstretched. "How do you do?" he said politely.

The Finger-eater! thought Gudrun and she remembered her parents' advice to put her hands in her pockets and run. But I won't, she said to herself bravely, for now may be my only chance to make the Finger-eater see how wrong it is to eat fingers. So she stood her ground.

"I'm sorry," she said, "but I cannot shake your hand because I'm holding this flask of milk."

"You could always hold it with your other hand," said Ulf, for it was he.

"I could," said Gudrun, "but I won't. I've heard of you, you see. You are Ulf the Finger-eater."

"Well, well," said Ulf, passing his tongue across his razor-sharp teeth, "and what is your name, little girl?"

"It's Gudrun. Now let me tell you something, Ulf," she said. "Eating fingers is wrong."

A clever little miss, thought Ulf. How can I trick her? He sat down on a nearby tree-stump, and crossed one bow-leg over the other, looking serious and thoughtful.

"You're right, Gudrun," he said. "I'm wrong to eat people's fingers, I see that now. But at least give me a drink of milk."

And when she holds out the flask, he thought, I'll soon have one of those lovely little pink sausages!

"Not on your life," said Gudrun. "Thanks to you, both my mother and my father are short of a finger."

"How time flies!" said Ulf. "That must have been when I was a very young troll. I've probably had a hundred fingers since then."

"Well, you're not having a hundred and one," said Gudrun, "but on second thoughts I'll give you that drink," and, pulling out the cork, she jerked the flask so that the milk shot out straight into Ulf's frog-face and, as he stood gasping, she dashed away.

Gudrun did not tell her parents of her meeting with Ulf. She simply said she had tripped, the cork had come out of the flask, and the milk had all spilled (a white lie, she told herself). But she continued to think long and hard about the Finger-eater. Somehow or other he must be made to give up his horrid habit.

Then one day Gudrun had a sudden, brilliant idea.

She was sitting outside the family tent, playing with a reindeer antler. This was the time of year when all the reindeer (for the cows are horned as well as the bulls) shed their antlers before growing fresh ones, and they were lying about everywhere. Hard as iron they were, and many of them were of the strangest shapes, for reindeer antlers are very large and many-pointed, those of some of the bulls curving right round and down until they almost meet the animals' faces.

The single antler that Gudrun held was quite a small one, probably from a young beast, but at its tip it had an odd shape, something like a human hand. It had at its end a flat surface resembling the palm of a hand and from this surface five points protruded. Just like four fingers and a thumb, thought Gudrun, and that was when the idea hit her.

That afternoon Ulf emerged from his hole to see Gudrun approaching, her long blonde plait swinging as she walked, her cornflower-blue eyes sparkling, her right hand, much to the troll's surprise, already outstretched in greeting. Admittedly she was wearing a large pair of reindeer hide gloves, but those won't save her, thought Ulf.

He advanced to meet her.

"Hello, Ulf," said Gudrun brightly. "I've come to say I'm sorry for throwing the milk at you. Will you shake hands and then we can be friends?"

Stupid child, thought Ulf. She's asking for it. This time I won't just have one finger, I'll have all four, and he grabbed Gudrun's right hand and shoved it into his frog-mouth and bit it as hard as he could.

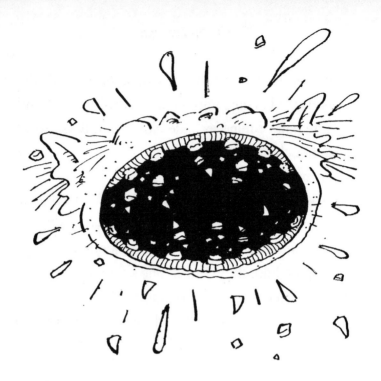

Then Ulf's great cry of agony echoed and rang from the circling hills, as his razor-sharp teeth broke and smashed and shattered, every one.

And Gudrun drew off the mangled glove that had concealed the antler, its stem thrust up the sleeve of her blouse, and revealed that bony five-pointed end that had looked so like a hand.

"Hard luck, Ulf," she said. "You bit off more than you could chew."

"Oh! Oh!" moaned the Finger-eater. "My teeth! My teeth! Every single one is loose in my head! Oh, it is agony! Help me! Help me!"

"I will," said Gudrun, and she took from the pocket of her skirt a pair of stout pliers, a useful tool with which her father was wont to draw stones that had lodged deep between the great splay hooves of his reindeer.

"Open wide, Ulf," she said, "and I'll make you a much better troll."

Then with the pliers she pulled out the teeth of the Finger-eater, one by one, till none were left.

Even after that, Ulf could not easily rid himself of his bad habit. Once his mouth was no longer sore, he still tried several times to live up to his name, but thanks to Gudrun, he could not. For though the reindeer can grow new antlers, hill-folk cannot grow new teeth, and those few people whose hands he caught only giggled at the harmless pressure of his toothless gums upon their fingers and told him not to be such a silly old troll.

So that before long Ulf fell into a terrible sulk, and disappeared down his hole in the hill, and was never seen again.

And even today, if you travel in the cold old North and stay amongst the reindeer people, you may hear the tale of the troll named Ulf and the girl called Gudrun, and how she and she alone put paid to the wicked ways of the Finger-eater.

Little Obie and the Flood

by MARTIN WADDELL
illustrated by ELSIE LENNOX

Little Obie lived with his grandad, Obadiah, and his grandma, Effie, in their cabin at Cold Creek, on the Rock River. It was lonely up there, but they liked it.

One day Grandad hitched up the wagon and took Obie down to Bailey's Ford, at the end of Big Valley. They stopped three miles down the track to pick up Wally Stinson, their next-door neighbour. He came with them on the wagon.

Bailey's Ford was the biggest place around. There were eight cabins there, and Hannigan's Store. Grandad drove to the store and they picked up the provisions. Little Obie and Wally Stinson helped Grandad load the wagon.

"Looks like bad weather's coming," said Mr Hannigan.

"Yep," said Grandad.

"Rain on the ridge," said Wally Stinson. "I never saw the mountains that black before."

"We'd best be getting back," said Grandad.

That was all he said, but it was enough to make Little Obie think a bit. Grandad never said a lot, that wasn't his way, nor Effie's either, but when he did say something, he meant it. It wasn't just talk.

It began to rain on the way back to Stinson's. Wally Stinson and Little Obie got under the canvas, but Grandad got wet up front driving. The wind and the rain lashed at the canvas, and it was very cold. It was dark when they got to Stinson's cabin.

"Stay awhile," said Mrs Stinson.

"Better get back to Effie," Grandad said. "River'll be rising in the creek."

This time, Little Obie knew Grandad was really worried. He lay in the back of the wagon as it lurched through the rain, and listened to the roar.

The roar was coming from Cold Creek. The water was rushing and rising. It gurgled round the wagon wheels as they forded the creek, and every minute it rose higher and higher as the rain poured down.

"Never saw the creek so high before, Effie," said Grandad, when they were back in the cabin.

"That's so," said Effie.

"I reckon you should look a few things out just in case we need to be moving," said Grandad.

"Maybe so," said Effie.

"I'm afraid," said Little Obie.

"Now see what you've done with your talk!" Effie said to Grandad. She hugged Obie close. Effie was long and thin, but her body was strong as whipcord. She wanted to give Little Obie some of her strength in case he'd need it, and that was why she hugged him.

Little Obie went to bed, but he didn't get any sleep because of the rain drumming on the roof, the water roaring in the creek and the noise of Grandad and Grandma shifting things below.

"You asleep, Little Obie?" Grandad said.

"No!" said Little Obie, sitting up in bed.

"We'd best be moving," said Grandad.

"Where are we going?" asked Little Obie.

"To the high ground," said Grandad.

They didn't want to be drowned in the rising water, so they had to move fast. They went in the wagon with all the things that would fit piled up on it. Effie drove the wagon and Grandad drove the animals. Little Obie kept in under the canvas, cold and wet and scared out of his skin.

They made it up as far as the high ground beyond

the creek, and there they slept, huddled together in the wagon for warmth and comfort.

When Little Obie woke the next morning, there was water everywhere, right down Big Valley. The creek had disappeared, and so had their cabin. It just wasn't there any more.

"Oh!" said Little Obie.

"Don't be afraid, Little Obie," said Grandad. "The water has risen and the river has burst its banks, but the water will go down again."

"Where's our cabin?" said Little Obie.

"Reckon it just washed away!" said Effie.

"What about the Stinsons?" said Little Obie.

"They should be all right," said Grandad. "It's the folks down the bottom of the valley will get the worst of it."

That started Little Obie thinking.

"What about Marty Hansen and her Pa?" he said. "And Mr Hedger, and Old Gerd Weber?"

Effie looked at Grandad, and Grandad didn't say a word. He just shook his head very slowly.

"Reckon they'll have got their feet wet," said Effie, but like always it wasn't what she said that Obie listened to, it was how she said it. Her eyes were glistening with tears. But then she wiped her nose,

86

and that dried her up, and she was old stiff-backed Effie again.

"We ought to go and see what happened to them," Little Obie said anxiously. Marty Hansen was his friend and he was worried about her.

"Nobody is going anywhere till the water goes down," said Grandad. "Specially not down the valley. There's no way we'd get the wagon through."

"Maybe Marty got drowned," said Little Obie.

Grandad and Effie didn't say a thing. There wasn't anything they could say.

It rained all day and the next night too, and then the rain stopped. But the water didn't go away. It kept coming off the mountain and rushing down the valley, and the trees and all went with it.

Then the water started to go down.

It went down all the next day, and the next, and then Grandad said they could try moving down the valley and see how far they could get.

There wasn't anything much left on the low ground but mud and broken trees. They had to lighten the wagon, and even then it sank in deep and they had to move the mud to get it out again, but in the end they made it down to where Bailey's Ford used to be.

Bailey's Ford nearly wasn't there. Most of it had

been swept away. But people had come to Bailey's Ford because there was no other place to go.

Old Gerd Weber and the Stinsons and Mr Hedger were there and the Currans and Mr Hannigan, and some of the other folk from the low ground came straggling in, but Marty Hansen and her Pa didn't come.

"Where's Marty?" Little Obie asked.

"Nobody has seen the Hansens," Wally Stinson said. "There's no getting down to their part of the valley yet."

"I want to go and find Marty, Grandad," Little Obie said.

"We'll go and look for Marty as soon as we can, Obie," said Grandad. "But there's things that have to be done here first."

They did the things. Little Obie kept thinking about Marty, but he had to be busy too, clearing away the mud and trying to build things up again. There just wasn't any crying time to spare.

"Maybe ... maybe Marty and her Pa went somewhere else?" Little Obie said to Grandad when they were fixing the stall for Curran's hogs.

"Maybe," said Grandad.

"And maybe not," said Effie, hammering away at

her stake. It was a cruel thing to say, but Effie didn't mean it that way. She thought Marty was dead, and Little Obie would have to face up to it, and get on with living with the folks who were left.

"Wally Stinson and me will go down the valley in the morning, Little Obie," Grandad said that night.

"I want to go too," said Little Obie.

"You're staying put," said Effie. "It's no business for a child."

Little Obie wasn't staying put.

Little Obie wasn't made that way.

The next morning when Grandad and Wally Stinson went in the wagon, Little Obie went too. Nobody knew he was going because he went in the back of the wagon under the straw.

Effie would have skinned him if she'd known.

There was still a lot of water swirling about the dip in the land down by the rock ridge, where Hansen's place used to be.

There was no cabin.

There was nothing much, just mud and broken trees, trapped against the ridge, where the water had left them.

"That's the end of the Hansens," Grandad said to Wally. "Little Obie will be real upset."

"Old Hansen and that girl, Marty," said Wally Stinson. "Reckon they never knew what hit them."

Little Obie lay there in the straw, with his feelings all huddled up inside, thinking about Marty and her Pa in the water.

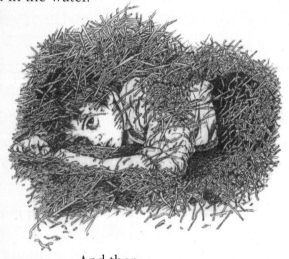

And then…

"Look there!" Little Obie heard Wally Stinson say.

The next minute Wally and Grandad were off the wagon down in the mud, heading for the rocks, and Little Obie was off after them. Only when he jumped off the wagon he fell down in the mud and it was over him, face and all. Then he dragged himself up and tried to run like a little mudball on legs and there was Grandad holding something limp in his arms, dirt-caked and bloody.

"Marty!" Little Obie said.

"Looks like we got here too late," Wally Stinson said.

But Grandad didn't pay any heed. He was holding Marty close and talking to her, trying to make her alive.

Then Marty opened her eyes and looked at Grandad and Obie. She looked as if she could see them, but she didn't show any sign that she knew who they were, or where she was, or what was happening.

She was like that all the way back in the wagon. Wally Stinson made Little Obie stay up front, and Grandad sat in the straw, hugging Marty to keep what life she had left in her after eight days in the wet and cold.

Little Obie wanted to help Marty, but he didn't know what to do, and in the end he just sat tight, close up to Wally at the front. Wally said Marty's Pa was dead, and they'd all have to be good to Marty because she would hurt a lot, and maybe they were too late and she would die too, but they'd have to pray that she didn't.

When they got back to Bailey's Ford, Effie and Mrs Stinson took Marty away to Mr Hannigan's bed by the stove in the room behind the store.

Marty just lay there and people took turns watching her, even Little Obie.

"Grandma?" said Little Obie one day. "Marty's Pa's dead."

"Reckon so," said Effie.

"What's going to happen to Marty?" asked Little Obie.

"She'd best come with us," said Effie. "If she gets better."

"I reckon she will," said Little Obie.

And Little Obie was right.

That's how Marty came to Cold Creek, to live with Little Obie.

Effie and Grandad and Marty and Little Obie rebuilt the cabin, only this time they built it up on the high ground, overlooking the creek.

"In case the water comes again," Grandad told Little Obie. "Next time we don't want to get our feet wet!"

Sky Watching

by DYAN SHELDON
illustrated by GRAHAM PERCY

Once upon a time,
there was a little girl
called Nancy. Nancy
wasn't a bad little
girl, but she was
easily bored.
No matter what
Nancy played
with, or what
she did, she
soon grew tired
of it. Then she
crossed her arms
and stamped her
foot. She scowled
and threw things
round the room.

"This is no fun any more!" cried Nancy. "I've got nothing to do! I'm bored, bored, bored!"

To stop Nancy from being bored, her parents bought her things.

"We'll buy you so many toys that you'll never be bored again," they promised.

They bought her everything they could think of: games and bicycles; balls and building blocks and model trains; storybooks and colouring pens and tiny planes that really flew; bags of stuffed animals and boxes full of smiling dolls.

Nancy crossed her arms and stamped her foot. She scowled. "I'm still bored," said Nancy.

Soon, Nancy had so many things that she had no more room for them.

If you squeezed through the door of Nancy's bedroom there was nowhere to walk. If you pushed your way to the bed there was nowhere to sit. If you opened the cupboard, toys fell on your head.

"I'm still bored," said Nancy. Her parents bought her more toys.

Soon Nancy had so many things that there was no more room in the house at all.

The sofa disappeared under a mountain of games. The kitchen table vanished beneath a sea of books. There were so many toys in the hall that Nancy's gran, who had come for a visit, got lost walking through the front door.

Nancy stamped her foot. There were plenty of things to throw, but nowhere to throw them. "I'm still bored," scowled Nancy. "I'm very, very bored."

Nancy's parents didn't know what to do.

"What shall we do?" asked Nancy's father.

"What *can* we do?" asked Nancy's mother.

"I'll tell you what I'd do," said a small, faraway voice.

Nancy's parents looked at one another.

"Who said that?" asked Nancy's parents.

"I said that!" snapped the small, faraway voice. A bony hand appeared from under a pile of dolls and teddy bears. It was Nancy's gran.

Everyone had forgotten about her, she'd been lost for so long. Nancy's parents helped her out.

"What *would* you do?" Nancy asked her grandmother. "Send me to bed without any supper?"

"Then you'd be hungry as well as bored," said Nancy's gran.

Nancy crossed her arms. "Are you going to stop me from watching telly?"

"No one's seen the telly in weeks," said Nancy's gran. "There wouldn't be much point in that."

Nancy stamped her foot. "I know!" cried Nancy. "You're going to take away all my toys!"

"What for?" asked her grandmother. "You don't play with them anyway."

Nancy frowned. "Well, if you're not doing any of those things, what are you going to do?"

Nancy's gran climbed down from the hillock of bicycles she'd been sitting on. "I'm going to make

you sit in the sky until you've learned your lesson," she said.

Nancy wasn't too keen on sitting in the sky.

What could be more boring than that?

"There's nothing to do in the sky," she complained.

Nancy's gran brought out a ladder. "Nothing?" she asked.

"Nothing," said Nancy.

"Then just look," said Nancy's gran.

Nancy scowled. "But there's nothing to look at."

Gran gave her a shove up the ladder. "I'm sure you'll find something," she said, pulling the ladder away.

Nancy sat down on a cloud and began to cry.

After a while she grew tired of crying when there was no one to hear her and beg her to stop.

"This isn't any fun," she sniffed. "Crying is boring, too."

She leaned over a cloud and called to her grandmother. "Can I come down now?" she asked. "I'm sure I've learned my lesson."

Nancy's gran appeared on the lawn. She was riding Nancy's skateboard. "What do you see in the sky?" she asked.

"Clouds," answered Nancy. "Lots of clouds."

"And what do they look like?" asked her gran.

"They're white," said Nancy. "They're big and white."

Her grandmother frowned. "You're not ready yet," she said and she rolled back into the house.

Nancy watched the sky a little more closely after that. There was certainly nothing else to do.

A flock of birds hurried by. I wonder where they're going, thought Nancy. Maybe they'll land under a palm tree on a tropical island.

Maybe they'll land in a colony of penguins at the South Pole.

Someone waved to Nancy from a passing plane.

Nancy waved back.

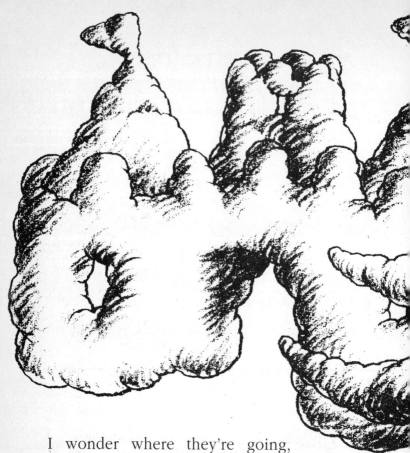

I wonder where they're going, thought Nancy. Maybe they were going to Europe, or Africa. Maybe they were going to the very top of the world.

As she watched the sky, Nancy noticed that not all of the clouds were white. Some were pink, or purple, or even green.

"Wow!" said Nancy. "Green clouds. They're great."

And not all of the clouds looked like clouds. A gigantic castle hung over Nancy's house. A family of dinosaurs floated past her head.

"Hey!" shouted Nancy, ducking out of the way. "There goes a brontosaurus!"

Night fell. Nancy's gran came out into the garden on Nancy's pogo stick.

"Nancy!" she shouted. "Nancy! Are you still there?"

Nancy peered over a giant turkey. "Here I am!" called Nancy. "I've been sliding on the clouds."

"It's getting late," said Nancy's grandmother. "Have you learned your lesson yet?"

Nancy blinked in surprise. She'd been so busy that she hadn't realized how dark it was. Suddenly, she wanted to be in her nice warm house, having her tea. "Oh, yes," said Nancy. "I'm sure I've learned my lesson. The sky isn't boring at all. It's filled with all sorts of interesting things. Can I come down?"

"Not so fast!" said Nancy's grandmother. "First tell me what you see now."

Nancy looked around. "I see the moon and stars," said Nancy.

"And what do they look like?" asked her gran.

Nancy shrugged. "They don't look like anything," said Nancy. "Just the moon and stars."

Nancy's gran sighed. "You're not ready yet," she said and she hopped back into the house.

Nancy sat down. She stared into the night.

Twinkle, twinkle little star, thought Nancy, what a boring star you are.

And then, out of the corner of her eye, Nancy saw something move. She turned her head.

"Look at that!" cried Nancy. "It's a bear! A giant bear made out of stars!"

Nancy was so excited she got to her feet. "And look at that! Starfish swimming in a river of moonlight!" The bear leaned down and dipped his paw in the river. The fish scattered in a shower of stars.

Nancy turned her head again. "And there's an eagle!" yelled Nancy. "And a hunter with a bow and arrow!" The hunter raised his bow. Nancy started jumping up and down. "Watch out!" she screamed. The eagle rose. "Wow!" laughed Nancy. "This is better than telly."

*   *   *

Nancy was playing hide-and-seek with the moon when her gran called her.

Nancy and the moon both looked down on Nancy's gran. She was riding one of Nancy's bikes.

"What is it?" asked Nancy.

"Your tea's ready," said her gran.

"Tea?" Nancy repeated. She'd forgotten about tea. "But I want to stay here. I'm having fun."

"Then you've learned your lesson," said her gran. "It's time to come down."

"But I'll be bored again," said Nancy.

Nancy's gran held out her arms for Nancy to jump.

"Oh, you won't be bored, you've got plenty to do," said Nancy's gran. "You have a houseful of toys to give away."

Tigers Forever

by RUSKIN BOND
illustrated by VALERIE LITTLEWOOD

On the left bank of the river Ganges, where it flows out from the Himalayan foothills, is a long stretch of forest. At one time this forest provided a home for some thirty to forty tigers, but men in search of skins and trophies had shot them all, and now there was only one old tiger left.

Although the tiger had passed the prime of his life, he had lost none of his majesty. His muscles rippled beneath the golden yellow of his coat, and he walked through the long grass with the confidence of one who knew that he was still a king, although his subjects were fewer. His great head pushed through the foliage, and it was only his tail, swinging high, that sometimes showed above the sea of grass.

One day, the tiger headed for the water of a large marsh, where he sometimes went to drink or cool off. The marsh was usually deserted except when buffaloes from the nearby village were brought there to bathe or wallow in the muddy water.

The tiger waited in the shelter of a rock, his ears pricked for any unfamiliar sound. Then he walked into the water and drank slowly.

Suddenly the tiger raised his head and listened, one paw suspended in the air. A strange sound had come to him on the breeze, so he moved swiftly into the shelter of the tall grass that bordered the marsh, and climbed a hillock until he reached his favourite rock. This rock was big enough to hide him and to give him shade.

The sound he had heard was only a flute, sounding thin and reedy in the forest. It was played by Nandu, a slim brown boy on a buffalo,

leading a herd of seven others. Chottu, a slightly smaller boy, rode at the back.

The tiger had often seen them at the marsh, and he was not bothered by their presence. He knew the village folk would leave him alone as long as he did not attack their buffaloes. And as long as there were deer in the forest, he would not need to.

He decided to move on and find a cool shady place on the hillock in the heart of the forest, where he could rest during the hot afternoon and be free of the flies and mosquitoes that swarmed around the marsh. At night he would hunt.

With a lazy grunt that was half a roar, "A-oonh!" – he got off his haunches and sauntered off. The gentlest of tigers' roars can be heard a kilometre away, and the boys looked up immediately.

"There he goes!" said Nandu, taking the flute from his lips and pointing with it towards the hillock. "Did you see him?"

"I saw his tail, just before he disappeared. He's a big tiger!"

"Don't call him tiger. Call him Uncle."

"Why?" asked Chottu.

"Because it's unlucky to call a tiger a tiger. My father told me so. But if you meet a tiger, and call him Uncle, he will leave you alone."

"I see," said Chottu. "You have to make him a relative. I'll try and remember that."

The buffaloes were now well into the marsh, and some of them were lying down in the mud. Buffaloes love soft wet mud and will wallow in it for hours. Nandu and Chottu were not so fond of the mud, so they went swimming in deeper water. Later, they rested in the shade of an old silk-cotton tree. It was evening, and the twilight fading fast, when the buffalo herd finally made its way homeward.

At dawn next day Chottu was in the forest on his own, gathering mahua flowers, to be made into jam. Bears like mahua flowers too, and will eat them straight off the tree.

Chottu climbed a large mahua tree and began breaking off the white flowers and throwing them to the ground. He had been in the tree for about five minutes when he heard the sound made by a bear – a sort of whining grumble – and presently a young bear ambled into the clearing beneath the tree.

It was a small bear, little more than a cub, and Chottu was not frightened. But he knew the mother bear might be close by, so he decided to take no chances and sat very still, waiting to see what the bear would do. He hoped it wouldn't choose the same tree for a breakfast of mahua flowers.

At first the young bear put his nose to the ground and sniffed his way along until he came to a large ant-hill. Here he began huffing and puffing, making the dust from the ant-hill fly in all directions. Bears love eating ants! But he was a disappointed bear, because the ant-hill had been deserted long ago. And so, grumbling, he made his way across to a wild plum tree. Shinning rapidly up the smooth trunk, he was soon perched in the upper branches. It was only then that he saw Chottu.

The bear at once scrambled several feet higher up the tree and laid himself out flat on a branch. It wasn't a very thick branch and left a large expanse of bear showing on either side. He tucked his head away behind another branch and, so long as he could not see the boy, seemed quite satisfied that he was well hidden, though he couldn't help grumbling with anxiety. Like most animals, he could smell humans, and he was afraid of them.

Bears, however, are also very curious. And

slowly, inch by inch, the young bear's black snout appeared over the edge of the branch. Immediately he saw Chottu, he drew back with a jerk and his head was once more hidden.

The bear did this two or three times, and Chottu, now greatly amused, waited until it wasn't looking, then moved some way down the tree. When the bear looked up again and saw that the boy was missing, he was so pleased with himself that he stretched right across to the next branch, to get at a plum. Chottu chose this moment to burst into laughter.

The startled bear tumbled out of the tree, dropped through the branches and landed with a thud in a heap of dry leaves.

And then several things happened at almost the same time.

The mother bear came charging into the clearing. Spotting Chottu in the tree, she reared up on her hind legs, grunting fiercely.

It was Chottu's turn to be startled. There are few animals more dangerous than a rampaging mother bear, and the boy knew that one blow from her clawed forepaws could finish him.

But before the bear reached the tree, there was

a tremendous roar, and the tiger bounded into the clearing. The bears turned and ran, the younger one squealing with fright. The tiger had been asleep nearby and the noise had woken him, putting him in a very bad mood.

He looked up at the trembling boy, and roared again.

Chottu nearly fell out of the tree.

"Good-day to you, Uncle," he stammered, grinning nervously.

With a low growl, the tiger turned his back on Chottu and walked away, his tail twitching with annoyance. How dare that whipper-snapper of a boy call him Uncle! Now he'd have to protect the scrawny child, he supposed…

Emily's Own Elephant

by PHILIPPA PEARCE
illustrated by JOHN LAWRENCE

Emily lived with her mother and father in a little
house in the corner of a big meadow. A river ran
along one side of the meadow.

Huge trees grew in the meadow. There were
oaks and chestnuts and sycamore and ash-trees.
Emily's father used to say, "There are far too many
trees in the meadow. Perhaps I should cut some of
them down."

127

His wife said, "You haven't enough to do in your spare time. That's why you want to go cutting trees down."

A big shed stood in the meadow. It was old, but it was not in ruins. There were no holes in the roof for the rain to come through. There were no holes in the walls for the wind to blow through. The shed was quite empty. It was not used for anything.

Emily's father said, "Perhaps I should pull that useless shed down."

Emily's mother said, "You haven't enough to do in your spare time. That's why you want to go pulling sheds down."

Emily said, "Don't cut the trees down. Don't pull the shed down. You never know when we may need trees and an empty shed."

Emily's father promised not to cut down the trees or pull down the shed just yet.

Emily visits the zoo

One day in winter Emily went to London to visit the Zoo. She went with her mother. They saw all the animals that Emily liked best: the lions, the tigers, the hippos, the rhinos, the camels, the giraffes, the elephant, the wolves and the panda-bear.

Then it was time for tea, and they went to the cafeteria. Emily's mother had a pot of tea and a packet of biscuits, and Emily had an ice-cream and a packet of potato crisps.

When they had finished tea, Emily's mother said, "It's nearly time to go home. Is there anything else you very much want to see, Emily?"

129

"Yes," said Emily. "I want to go to the Children's Zoo."

So they went to the Children's Zoo. They saw the rabbits and Emily stroked one. They watched the chickens hatching out of eggs.

They visited the goats, and Emily fed one with a sandwich, and then it ate the paper-bag, and then it tried to eat the glove on the hand that had held the sandwich and the paper-bag.

Then Emily and her mother came to a special enclosure with a baby elephant in it. It was the nicest elephant that Emily had ever seen.

A keeper was standing by the elephant's enclosure. Emily asked him, "What is the baby elephant called?"

"Jumbo," said the keeper.

"Jumbo!" said Emily's mother. "What a nice name! Now, Emily, it's time to go home."

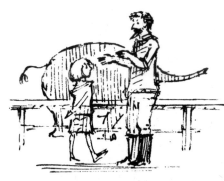

The keeper said to Emily, "We are very worried about Jumbo."

"Why?" said Emily.

"Come along, Emily," said her mother.

The keeper said to Emily, "We are worried about Jumbo because he doesn't grow. He is strong and he is healthy, but he simply won't grow. He is going to be a miniature elephant."

"I didn't know that elephants could be miniature," said Emily.

"*Come along, Emily,*" said her mother.

"It happens only very, very rarely," said

131

the keeper. "But it is always very awkward. The Zoo wants only elephants that are elephantine in size. It can't keep a miniature elephant."

"Oh," said Emily.

"COME ALONG, EMILY," said her mother.

"We shall have to find a home for Jumbo," said the keeper.

"EMILY!" said Emily's mother very loudly and crossly.

Emily usually did what her mother told her, especially as her mother usually told her to do only sensible things. So now Emily began to follow her mother out of the Children's Zoo.

Then Emily stopped. "I'm sorry," she said to her mother, "but we can't go home yet. I have an important idea. I must discuss it with the keeper. I must go back now."

So back they went.

The plan

They went back to the baby elephant's enclosure. The keeper was still standing there. He was looking at Jumbo in a worried way.

Emily said, "You told us that you would have to find a home for Jumbo."

"Yes," said the keeper.

"We could give him a home," said Emily, and she looked at her mother.

Emily's mother said to the keeper, "My daughter is quite right. We should be delighted to give your

little elephant a home."

The keeper said, "That's very kind of you; but even a miniature elephant needs a great deal of space."

"Would a big meadow do?" asked Emily's mother.

"A really big meadow," said Emily.

"Yes," said the keeper, "a really big meadow would do. But even a miniature elephant needs a lot of water to drink and to bathe in and to squirt around when it plays."

"Would a river running by the meadow do?" Emily asked.

"Yes," said the keeper, "a river would do. But what about when it rains – what about when it rains bucketfuls and blows gales? The little elephant will need shelter then."

"Would a shed in the meadow do?" asked Emily.

"A really big shed," said her mother. "It has no holes in the roof or the walls and it's quite empty."

"Yes," said the keeper, "a really big shed would do."

"Then that's settled," said Emily's mother.

"Wait!" said the keeper. "What about when it snows and freezes: would your shed be warm enough for a little elephant then?"

"No," said Emily. "Our shed hasn't a coal fire; it

hasn't a gas fire; it hasn't an electric fire."

"Wait," said Emily's mother. "We could put in central heating."

"Wouldn't that be very expensive?" said Emily.

"It would probably be worth it," said her mother. "It's not often anyone has the chance of a baby elephant that will stay small."

"That's settled then," said the keeper. "We are very

grateful to you. There's just one more thing."

"What is that?"

"Jumbo will be lonely without any of his friends," said the keeper. "Could you take one of his friends as well?"

"What kind of friend?" asked Emily's mother.

"His best friend is a baby monkey called Jacko. He likes climbing," said the keeper.

"Then he can climb all the trees in the meadow," said Emily's mother.

"I've always longed for a little elephant and a monkey," said Emily.

"When they are old enough," said the keeper, "Jumbo and Jacko will come to you in a special Zoo van. Please write your name and address on this piece of paper."

So they did, and then they went home.

Friends in the meadow

One day in summer Emily's father was eating toast and marmalade and looking out of the window.

Suddenly he spoke with his mouth full, "There is a big van, like a horse-box, at the gate into our meadow. Two men are driving the van into our meadow. Now they are opening the van. Something is coming out. *Oh! Oh! Oh!*"

Emily's father nearly choked on his toast and marmalade. He said, "There is an elephant in our meadow, with a monkey on its back!"

Then Emily and her mother told him all about Jumbo and Jacko. They had been keeping the secret to surprise him.

He was delighted. He said, "We must be sure to have the central heating in the shed before next winter. I will put it in myself. That will save expense."

"It will also give you something to do in your spare time," said his wife.

Then they all went into the meadow with buns for the elephant and bananas for the monkey. They took a pot of tea for the Zoo men, and a big plum cake

that happened to be in the house. There was a slice for everybody and sugar biscuits too, and chocolate fingers. They all had a picnic together in the sunshiny meadow.

Then the Zoo men said goodbye and went home. Emily's mother went indoors to make more buns. Emily's father went up the village to the public library to borrow a book about central heating.

Emily was left alone in the meadow with Jumbo and Jacko. It was very hot, so Emily led the way to the river. Jumbo waded in the cool water and squirted it over his friends. They loved this.

Then Jacko went racing through the treetops. He picked armfuls of pink and white blossom from the

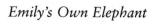

very tops of the chestnut-trees. It was
the biggest and best chestnut
blossom that Emily had ever seen.
She made wreaths and garlands
and chains of it for Jumbo and
Jacko and herself.

Then they began to dance round and round and
round the meadow. Emily's mother finished baking
her buns and came into the meadow to watch.
Emily's father came home with his book on central

heating and went into the meadow too. Emily's father and mother stood and watched and laughed and clapped. And round and round the meadow danced Emily and her two friends from the Zoo.

Acknowledgements

Art, You're Magic!
Text © 1992 Sam McBratney Illustrations © 1992 Tony Blundell

"Vicky Fox" from *Willa and Old Miss Annie*
Text © 1994 Berlie Doherty Illustrations © 1994, 1995 Kim Lewis

"Shaleen Goes Swimming" from *Imran's Secret*
Text © 1990 Nadya Smith Illustrations © 1995 Roberta Mansell

The Finger-eater
Text © 1992 Dick King-Smith Illustrations © 1992 Arthur Robins

"Little Obie and the Flood" from *Little Obie and the Flood*
Text © 1991 Martin Waddell Illustrations © 1991 Elsie Lennox

Sky Watching
Text © 1992 Dyan Sheldon Illustrations © 1992 Graham Percy

"Tigers Forever" from *Tiger Roars, Tiger Soars*
Text © 1983 Ruskin Bond Illustrations © 1983 Valerie Littlewood

Emily's Own Elephant
Text © 1987 Philippa Pearce Illustrations © 1987 John Lawrence